EPB
ARNOLD Parts
PARTS

Arnold, Tedd.

DISCARDED
Huron Public Library

Parts

For Mike, John, Fred,
Matt, Phil, and Ryan

Keep it together, guys!

PUFFIN BOOKS
Published by the Penguin Group
Penguin Putnam Books for Young Readers, 345 Hudson Street, New York, New York 10014, U.S.A.
Penguin Books Ltd, 27 Wrights Lane, London W8 5TZ, England
Penguin Books Australia Ltd, Ringwood, Victoria, Australia
Penguin Books Canada Ltd, 10 Alcorn Avenue, Toronto, Ontario, Canada M4V 3B2
Penguin Books (N.Z.) Ltd, 182-190 Wairau Road, Auckland 10, New Zealand

Penguin Books Ltd, Registered Offices: Harmondsworth, Middlesex, England

First published in the United States of America by Dial Books for Young Readers, a division of Penguin Putnam Inc., 1997
Published by Puffin Books, a division of Penguin Putnam Books for Young Readers, 2000

31 33 35 37 39 40 38 36 34 32

Copyright © Tedd Arnold, 1997
All rights reserved

THE LIBRARY OF CONGRESS HAS CATALOGED THE DIAL EDITION AS FOLLOWS:
Arnold, Tedd.
Parts / Tedd Arnold.—1st ed.
p. cm.
Summary: A five-year-old boy thinks his body is falling apart until
he learns that new teeth grow, and hair and skin replace themselves.
ISBN 0-8037-2040-8 (trade).—ISBN 0-8037-2041-6 (lib. bdg.)
[1. Body, Human—Fiction. 2. Stories in rhyme.] I. Title.
PZ8.3.A647Par 1997 [E]—dc20 96-28552 CIP AC

Puffin Books ISBN 978-0-140-56533-1

Printed in the United States of America

Except in the United States of America, this book is sold subject to the condition that it shall not,
by way of trade or otherwise, be lent, re-sold, hired out, or otherwise circulated without the publisher's
prior consent in any form of binding or cover other than that in which it is published and without
a similar condition including this condition being imposed on the subsequent purchaser.

Parts

Tedd Arnold

PUFFIN BOOKS

HURON PUBLIC LIBRARY
521 DAKOTA AVE S
HURON, SD 57350

I just don't know what's going on
Or why it has to be.
But every day it's something worse.
What's happening to me?

I think it was three days ago
I first became aware—
That in my comb were caught a couple
Pieces of my hair.

I stared at them, amazed, and more
Than just a bit appalled
To think that I was only five
And starting to go bald!

Then later on (I don't recall
Exactly when it was)
I lifted up my shirt and found
This little piece of fuzz.

I stared at it, amazed, and wondered,
What's this all about?
But then I understood. It was
My stuffing coming out!

Next day when I was outside playing
With the water hose,
I saw that little bits of skin
Were peeling from my toes.

I stared at them, amazed, and then
I gave a little groan,
To think that pretty soon I might
Be peeled down to the bone.

Then yesterday, before my bath,
As I took off my clothes,
A chunk of something gray and wet
Fell right out of my nose.

I stared at it, amazed, and thought,
I should be feeling pain.
Well, wouldn't *you* if you just lost
A little piece of brain?

So now, today, I'm sitting here
Enjoying Dr. Seuss,
And suddenly I realize
A tooth is coming loose!

I wiggle it, amazed, dismayed,
Too horrified to speak.
Without my teeth, how can I eat?
Already I feel weak!

Now I'm really worried. I'm
As scared as I can be,
'Cause finally what's happening
Is very clear to see—

The glue that holds
our parts together
isn't holding me!!!

And now I'm thinking to myself,
What's next in line to go?
Might be my ears; might be my eyeballs.
How's a kid to know?

HURON PUBLIC LIBRARY
521 DAKOTA AVE S
HURON, SD 57350

One day I might be playing ball...
And have my arm fall off.

Or maybe I could lose my head
If suddenly I cough.

Quite soon I'll be in pieces in
A pile without a shape.

Thank goodness Dad keeps lots and lots
And lots of masking tape.

What?

You forgot?
  To tell me teeth fall out?
And when they do, some brand-new teeth
  Will soon begin to sprout?

My hair, my skin, and everything—
There's nothing I should fear?

So all of me is normal. Whew!
That's really good to hear!

Then tell me, what's this yellow stuff
I got out of my ear?